BERLIN SYNDROME

Melanie Joosten's debut novel, *Berlin Syndrome*, saw her named a *Sydney Morning Herald* Best Young Novelist and receive the Kathleen Mitchell Award; it has since been made into a motion picture directed by Cate Shortland. In 2016, she published the essay collection *A Long Time Coming*. Her work appears in various publications, including *Meanjin*, *Kill Your Darlings*, *Best Australian Stories 2014*, and *Going Down Swinging*.

BERLIN SYNDROME

MELANIE JOOSTEN

SCRIBE
Melbourne • London

Scribe Publications
18-20 Edward St, Brunswick, Victoria 3056, Australia
2 John St, Clerkenwell, London, WC1N 2ES, United Kingdom

First published by Scribe 2011
This edition published 2017
Copyright © Melanie Joosten 2011

Typeset in 12.5/17.5 pt Granjon by the publishers.
Printed and bound in Australia by Griffin Press.

The paper this book is printed on is certified against the Forest
Stewardship Council® Standards. Griffin Press holds FSC
chain of custody certification SGS-COC-005088. FSC promotes
environmentally responsible, socially beneficial and economically
viable management of the world's forests.

Scribe Publications is committed to the sustainable use of natural resources and
the use of paper products made responsibly from those resources.

9781922070364 (Australian paperback)
9781925228663 (UK paperback)
9781921942051 (e-book)

A CiP data record for this title is available from the National Library of
Australia and the British Library.

scribepublications.com.au
scribepublications.co.uk

To my parents

I

Berlin is overrun by dogs. Every evening as she waits for Andi, Clare listens to their muffled barks drift over the walls and settle in the forgotten courtyard below. She taps out a tuneless beat on her bare thigh and waits for change, for movement. Somehow it is more difficult to imagine anything happening in the courtyard than it is to imagine the unseen dogs and their walkers nearby. Running her hands across her thighs, she reads the corrugated surfaces like braille. The inflammation has retreated, the cuts have become scabs, soon they will become scars. More lines will join these ones — her legs like furrowed fields waiting for the season to turn.

The days are getting longer. Or at least it is getting dark later. Running without pause into the next, the days do not seem particularly long or short. She has turned both of the clocks to face the wall; her watch battery is long dead. An overcast sky refuses to acknowledge that it might be spring while the sun, defeated by clouds, is too diffused to track across the surfaces of the apartment.

The plant must be growing. She looks at its leaves — does it realise that time has slowed? Its foliage clings to its stem, hoping for the sunlight to return. The leaves leave in winter. The leaves are left. Left is not right. She is left here; it is not right. The words thump at her temples, demanding her attention. Refusing to be pummelled into sentences, they want to stand on their own. The longer she spends here by herself, not talking, the louder the words seem to jostle about, wanting to be acknowledged. Why does 'left' mean two things? Why can it not just be one? 'Apple' means apple. It does not mean up or down. She paces the apartment. Step, step, step, turn. Faster and faster. She tries to walk in a straight line, careful not to lose her balance, careful not to lose her mind.

In the living room, she whirls around, tries to catch the plant watching her. It must be: she is the only other living thing in the apartment. They are attracted to each other, she and the plant, of that she is sure, but she is yet to garner proof.

As she pulls on her jeans, she feels she is part of a performance. The apartment is like a stage set, ready for the same action to be played out night after night. Each item of furniture is steeped in importance, heavy with meaning and signifying something — she is determined to find out exactly what.

She takes the clock from the bookshelf, turns it to face the room. Tick. Tick. That time is still passing is a relief. Step, step, step, turn. She paces the apartment, stretching her legs as though the more distance she covers, the faster time will pass. *Come home now, come home.* At last, the key in the lock, and she hurries to the hallway.

'Andi! Andi, you're home.'

Without saying hello, he dumps shopping bags at his feet, turns away from her and shuts the door. His hair and shoulders are wet. She had not noticed that it was raining. He picks up the bags, and as he walks past her into the kitchen, she reaches out to touch his hair, conjuring up some of the absent weather for herself.

'Andi?'

'What?' He places the shopping bags on the bench and moves past her to hang his jacket on the back of a dining chair.

'You're home.' She says it quietly, but her heart bats the statement about like a refrain. He is home, he is home.

He grunts an acknowledgement and begins unpacking the shopping. She watches as he stacks cans of chickpeas and tomatoes in the cupboard and posts vegetables into the refrigerator crisper. He empties a bag of apples into the fruit bowl and flings a loaf of bread against the toaster where it sighs as it settles.

'How was your day?'

The question rolls across the floor and stops at his feet. Nothing else moves inside the apartment.

'Andi?'

He continues to put the groceries away.

'Did something happen?'

'Nothing happened.'

'Is something wrong?' She waits in the doorway.

'Nothing is the matter, Clare!' His forehead pulls at his nose, his top lip snags above his teeth. 'I've been harassed by students all day, I don't need the same from you. Just leave me alone, would you?'

She takes a step back, but he steps towards her. She is getting it wrong; she should not have asked.

'Why do I have to come home to this? You're always here, Clare! You're making me nervous, watching me the way you do.' His face is above hers: it looks like it might fall on top of her, swallow anything she might say. 'I could end this, Clare. Anytime I want. You know that, don't you?'

She nods. And she wishes that he would.

~

The first time Clare left Andi, the sun hung low in its autumn hour. Long shadows enveloped buildings, and she watched as the streetlights began to flicker and turn on, one by one.

'Do you like strawberries?'

She looked across to see a man waiting, like her, for the traffic lights to change. He was tall with curly hair, and in his hand was a paper bag.

'Yes.' With one word she acquiesced to all that was to follow. The traffic lights changed with a commanding bleep, the pedestrians surged forth around them, and she picked a strawberry from the bag.

'Do you want to seat?'

'To sit?' she asked, looking about. There were no benches nearby.

'Yes.' He nodded enthusiastically, leading her to a pink pipe that ran above the footpath.

Clare was fascinated by these pipes that wound through the city, their brutal industrial appearance softened by the most feminine of colours. Were they an art installation, leading tourists to the Museumsinsel? Without a beginning or an end, these pipes snaked about the old East Berlin — around corners, high above roads, beneath raised footpaths. They were about the size of a dinner plate in diameter, maybe smaller. The various lengths were bolted together, sometimes in strange, convoluted arrangements as though the gods had sprayed the city with Silly String.

'Why are they pink?'

'Pink? The strawberries are red, no? *Rot*?' Confusion flailed on his face.

'I mean the pipes. Why are they pink?' She banged the heel of her hand against the pipe they were sitting on.

'Ah. I do not know exactly. Because pink means nothing, I suppose.'

'Pink means lots of things — little girls, breast cancer, pride.' Pink was possibly overladen with more meaning than any other colour. Except black. Or red. Scrolling through the colour spectrum, she concluded that most colours seemed overburdened with meaning.

'True,' he replied. 'But for the streets, pink means nothing. You do not usually see pink in the roadworks, the buildings, the landscape. It is bright, so it is obvious, and it makes even the hard-hatted feel joy.'

'The hard-*hearted*?'

'Yes!' He laughed loudly. 'My accent, I suppose? Hat, heart. You see, if the pipes were red, it would be alarming, one. And two, it would be Soviet — not good. And if they were green, they would get lost in the trees. Yellow, too bright in the sun, and blue? The ones up high would camouflage against the sky!' He was triumphant. 'So that is why the construction pipes are pink.'

'Construction pipes?'

'Yes. That is all they do in Berlin these days. They build, and they build, and they build. And Berlin, she is built on sand.

Every time they dig a basement, they sink the foundations and the water comes up. So the pipes take away the water.'

It was a wonderful thing, a city built on water. She came from a country where the cities settled on dust, the water long leached away, helped by an inexorable belief in the present and an unforgiving sun. Water restrictions obliged all of Melbourne's fountains to be switched off; the punitive shutting down of such follies a reprimand to a people who had turned a blind eye for so long that, by the time they looked back, water had become a privilege rather than a right. She considered the possibility of laying these pink pipes all the way to her thirsty hometown. It would be simpler to turn the world upside down.

'Many people think they are art.' He shook his head in mock consternation. 'So where are you from, that you do not have water pipes?'

'Melbourne.'

'I see — then you are far from home.'

They paused, each waiting for the other to say something, but she broke first. Starved of company after months travelling alone, she could not bear to let an opportunity for conversation pass her by. 'You are from Berlin?'

'Yes, I am. A true local. Though I must admit I do not spend much time in this part of the city, so do not ask me for directions.'

His was a voice worth pausing for, his turn of phrase was endearing. It tripped her up and made her aware of each word — alive to what he was saying, not just considering what she would say next. He asked what it was like in Australia, and she told him — the stock-standard descriptions at first, and then the real. They talked about places they had been and others

8

they would like to go, and she wondered at the way his brain could work in two languages while hers felt weighted down by one.

'Your English really is very good.' She plucked another strawberry from the bag, watching him closely. 'Do you always practise by chatting up foreigners?'

'Ha! You are very suspicious.' He pulled his attention from the milling tourists and turned his whole body towards her. 'I only wish I had such opportunity. But I am simply an English teacher at a high school. And so, sadly, I have more practice dealing with unruly students than women.' He held her gaze as he spoke, and she struggled to look away.

'So where are the strawberries from?' she asked. She could feel the heat of a blush wending its way to her cheeks and she bit her lip, willing it to subside.

'I grow them in my mother's *Schrebergarten*.' He looked at her to see if she understood. 'It is a little garden among many, on the outskirts of Berlin.' He gestured with his head, a throwaway nod. It seemed to indicate a place that was both close and yet very far away.

'I suppose it is really my father's now ...' His voice trailed off. 'However, I must go.' He stood up from the pipe and turned with his hand outstretched. 'My name is Andi.' His hand hovered before her, and she popped the last of the strawberry into her mouth so that she could shake it. Grasping her hand, he pulled her to her feet and kissed her with familiarity, once on each cheek.

This European gesture always took her by surprise, the brief brush of his lips plummeting her into an intimacy she had only ever found with old friends or whisky-soaked strangers in bars.

The scratch of his stubble gave her pause. In that short moment, with her own hand still encased in his, she was aware that it had been more than four months since somebody had touched her with any kind of intent.

'Clare,' she replied. The blush, too long held back, was set free, and desperate to keep him from seeing it, she leaned in and kissed him on the mouth. 'Pleased to meet you,' she said. And she walked away.

Clare is beautiful. This is a statement of fact, not an observation. Andi pictures himself in a courtroom, under oath and having to answer the questions thrown at him. *Describe her.* She is beautiful. She is small, but he expected her legs to be longer. Her smile is too wide for her face, and her hair is such a dark red it threatens to be brown. She is pretty, especially in her underwear. That, too, is a statement of fact, Your Honour. She looks so very fragile in her underwear, and he wishes he saw her like this more often. Soft and in need of protection. She cannot go out in the cold dressed like that. She cannot walk through the streets: her feet will numb, her lips will turn blue.

He watches her walk across the kitchen, take one mug at a time from the drying rack and hang each one on the row of hooks beneath the kitchen cabinets. Her legs swerve in at the knees. Ulrike had long, thin legs, but they didn't go in at the knees or the ankles. It made her seem doll-like, as though she was stuffed with balled cotton. Clare's legs do not suffer this misfortune, however, and they bend in to each other just a bit. Like a bird. When she reaches up to put the plates in the cupboard, she stands on one leg and the other flicks up behind.

He will buy her some new underwear. Something pink and flamingo-like. He smiles to himself, imagining already the delight on her face when he presents her with this gift. She loves presents. She appreciates them more obviously than anyone he has ever known. She insists on sitting down together to open any present, no matter how big or small, however serious or comedic. She will parade around the apartment, dressed in whatever he has bought, or immediately put it to use.

'What?' She turns to face him, cup in hand.

'Nothing,' he answers, innocent. He smiles at her: she looks so indignant.

'Why were you looking at me?'

'Because you look like a flamingo.'

She snorts dismissively and turns back to the dishes. He bets she is rolling her eyes at the cupboards. He is glad he did not simply say, 'Because you are beautiful.' She does not like it when he compliments her on her looks. She says it is bad manners to compliment someone on things they have no control over.

Restless, he wanders into the bedroom. When he is at work, or out shopping, or visiting his father, all he can think about is how he wants to be back here in the apartment with her. Yet when he is here, sometimes it is not quite as he remembers. In his daydreams, she wants everything he wants, does everything he says.

'Come to bed, baby,' he calls out to her.

He switches on the lamp, sits on the bed and takes off his shoes. He always thinks of his father when he sees his shoeless feet: they wear the same socks. When Andi was still living at home, they would sit together in the evenings, books open in their laps. His father's feet were large and docile, like big sleeping animals. They each liked to think they just had the television on for the comfort of sound, and that really they were immersed in their reading. Flipping the occasional page, they would furtively watch the television without comment.

'Clare?' She has not appeared in the doorway, and he cannot hear her moving about the apartment. Maybe she has fallen asleep on the couch; she is prone to doing that. And then she is grumpy when she wakes up, as though it is his fault she is so tired and he should never have let her fall asleep there. But it is not his fault. He makes sure she has plenty of time to rest.

He lets himself drop back on the bed, feet still on the floor. He stares up at the ceiling, which is interrupted by a lone globe. It used to wear a paper-lantern covering, but she removed it. She told him it was deceitful, as though it had something to hide, and that she would rather see the globe do what it was designed to do. He did not argue. He has learned when not to argue.

'Clare, baby, come to bed.'

No response. What is she doing? He clenches his fists and counts to three before pushing himself up off the bed and striding along the hallway. She is standing in the doorway of the living room. The backs of her hands are pressed against the doorframe.

'Look,' she says. She steps towards him, and her arms float up, like a slow-motion star jump. 'I can't stop them from moving,' she says, delighted. 'They just want to go up of their own accord.'

He reaches out and takes one of her hands, interrupting its ascent.

~

He was not really following her, he told himself, he was just curious to see where she was going. An anthropological study of a foreigner in Berlin. She had been reading on a park bench when he first saw her, a bag tucked beneath her head as a pillow. Something about her insouciance had caught his eye; she lay there as though she was in her own bedroom, oblivious to the square's activity — even to the school students who milled about on the steps of the concert hall, puncturing the air with their shoving and shouts. He was certain she was a foreigner: a local would have somewhere better to go, and she was not smoking.

He had stood at the edge of the square watching her. What was she doing here? What was anyone doing here? These were dead parts of the city — churches restored to eerie perfection, monuments erected to memories that had collapsed under the weight of more recent history. He felt as though the new century was hurtling forward, leaving nothing authentic in its place. He was supposed to meet his father to attend a public lecture on *ostalgie* — the nostalgia people felt for the East. As was so often the case, his father had lost track of time, had called to say he would meet Andi at the restaurant instead. Andi had been relieved: he was not in the mood to debate what was lost along with the past, and he had left the lecture hall and wandered down the street, looking for somewhere to catch the last of the day's sun. But every surface was covered with tourists clinging like brightly coloured lichen to their resting places. It was then that he had seen her, lying so still, unaware of the surrounding tumult and looking enviably content.

What would he have done if she had not liked strawberries? He had ducked into the minimart, and they had seemed the most appetising and least threatening of offerings. Never go anywhere empty-handed, his mother always said. When he came out of the store, he had experienced a moment of brief panic: the bench was bare. Spotting her nearing the intersection, he broke into a jog, arriving at her side to discover that she did like strawberries, and that she was from elsewhere — Australia. Where the people were laid back and had no worries. She even used that phrase. When she had asked where the strawberries were from, he had not wanted to disappoint her.

He followed her now as she walked down Friedrichstrasse, her hands in her pockets, and her bag hugging her back. He felt a little miffed that she did not look around, even though she did not know he was there. At Checkpoint Charlie she glanced at the hoarding that surrounded the empty lots, but must have decided to ignore its multilingual tourist information and walk on.

He should just catch up to her and ask for her number. But that would mean admitting he had followed her this far. Instead, he slowed his pace and watched as she turned the next corner and headed into a bookstore.

She had seemed to concentrate when he had spoken, to wait with a vicious intent, and he had found his English deserting him. She told him that she had been watching his city all day; an architectural photographer, she saw the city in cubes and planes, shapes and shadows. He liked the idea of her watching his city unfold, being made new again. Envying her freedom to observe, he had wanted to assure her that he, too, was an outsider looking in.

'Sometimes I like to just sit there and complicate the world.' He had watched for her reaction.

Clare had laughed, throwing her head back in a pantomime of enjoyment. Would it annoy him after some time? Would he stop trying to make her laugh?

'*Complicate*? You mean contemplate … but it's very funny.'

He had laughed with her. It was a good choice. He had almost gone with compensate. Consummate. Concentrate. Consecrate. Complicate had definitely been the best choice.

Resigning himself to being late for his father, Andi now followed her into the bookstore. Clare stopped at a shelf of art books and dropped to a crouch. She pulled out a book, and he squinted to see. Egon Schiele. She put it back, stood and looked about, as though assessing the store. Andi seized a book and kept himself hidden behind a shelf, feeling as if he was in a British comedy. What would he say if she saw him? Pretend it was a coincidence, that this was his favourite bookstore?

Clare possessed her body as if she was the only person in the room. How was it that nobody else was staring at her? She dropped to the floor again; he was so close he could hear her knees click. They made a popping sound, like the snapping of fingers calling attention. Surely everyone in the store was tracking her every move? She pulled a book on Klimt from the shelf and sat on the carpet of the shop, legs crossed, flipping the pages and tilting them away from the glare of the lights.

Andi's phone beeped. Its vibrations felt like a small animal impatiently pawing at his hip. He put the book down, still watching Clare, who was oblivious to the people who wanted to get past her. Again he almost stepped forward and asked for her number. He wanted to yell the request out at her, to see his words slam into her face and shake her from her reverie. But because he could not be sure that she would yell back, he left the store. He did not want to play with uncertainty.

As he walked to the restaurant, Andi wondered whether his father had missed the lecture on purpose. They had such different views of the past, particularly that of the GDR. His father saw it as something separate, another world that could not be understood by those who inhabited the present. Andi saw it as an extension of today: it could not all be shuffled out of sight, or forgiven. He had no idea what his mother thought of the past, if she thought of it at all.

Stepping into the fuggy air of the restaurant, Andi saw his father waiting for him at a table. Even when seated, he was a tall man. A man whose clothes floated about his body as though they were afraid to make contact, giving the impression of much broader shoulders — of much more man — than Andi's father could lay claim to.

He wondered whether he would have liked his father if they had met as friends of the same age. Probably not. And yet they recognised themselves in each other. The same nose, the same mouth. Their teeth were disorderly, their top lips curled in a way that could be perceived as endearing or unkind. Years ago, his father would host study groups in their apartment, and Andi would watch the discussion, unnoticed as voices were raised, ideas volleyed about. He saw how his father could sneer in a manner that made students look away, or be so charming that some of them, women and men, would blush. Andi spent many hours trying to emulate his father's magnetic scowl, but it always appeared self-conscious rather than disaffected. Somehow, this failure made him dislike his father and his easy manner all the more.

As his father stood, Andi was reminded how far into old age he had retreated. They muddled through their greetings, his father apologising again for missing the lecture as Andi awkwardly embraced him and sat down too quickly. They passed their conversation back and forth across the table, questions of work and study carrying them through to dessert. He found himself watching the clock on his phone, wishing his father didn't always make him want to be somewhere else.

'Your mother would like to see you.' His father poured water into his glass as he said this, his eyes following the stream. Andi surveyed his cutlery. The stainless-steel cake knife had fine scratches all over its surface; sweeping lines from edge to edge. Cloudy marks hovered where the soapy water had dried, a snail trail of detergent.

'Why?' He watched the hurt trickle across his father's face. Andi sighed. It was not his father he wanted to punish. But he was so easy to bruise; a word flung at high speed across the table, or even a lazy drop shot, was all it took.

'You're her son, Andreas. She wants to see you.'

He thought about not even saying the words: his father knew what his reply would be. 'I don't want to see her.'

His father nodded. And they sat in silence until Andi gestured for the bill.

Clare's left foot had gone to sleep. She closed the monograph and slid it back into its place on the shelf. Jiggling her leg until the numbness began to dissipate, she hauled herself up from the floor and looked towards the doorway. Night had completely fallen: she should head back to the hostel; she should get something to eat.

She wanted to do neither of these things; both seemed like insurmountable tasks. Sighing, she picked up her bag and left the store. She was tired of creating purpose for herself and ashamed at this tiredness. Could she not just enjoy this as a holiday? She walked a few paces towards Checkpoint Charlie, telling herself to join in, to queue in the gift store for an *Ampelmännchen* tea towel and fridge magnet, and to dash off witty postcards for friends back home. Instead she walked towards Potsdamer Platz, hoping the bustle and the shiny newness of it all would shake her out of her own weary mind. She wondered briefly what the man with the strawberries — Andi — was doing that night. She pictured him holding court in a bar, his audience's rapt attention, much as she imagined his students behaving, hanging from his every word. It seemed admirably useful — teaching a language, enabling people to communicate. And though she knew that photography played a similar role, that images could parade truth in a way that words never could, her career still seemed so futile.

When she decided to take this trip, she had been overjoyed to put all of her commercial work on hold, had not even bothered to give her clients a date of return. She was tired of the smoke and mirrors or, more accurately, the mirrors and Photoshop of architectural photography. The way the architects who employed her insisted the images be more than each building was, or ever could be. That the hero shot must show the structure thrusting into the city skyline, as though it was tearing a hole in the atmosphere, despite architecture in Australia only ever being deserving of the term 'tasteful'. Wanting to see buildings that were designed with purpose, she mapped out a trip through the former Eastern Bloc. In each city and town she found these buildings, most in a state of neglect, that spoke of the utopian future that never arrived. Strictly places in which to live and to work, they were designed as an extension of a collective, rather than a personal, identity. Yet she was under no illusions about the brutal nature of communism and its socialist sisters: she remembered watching the ABC news as a child, seeing people dancing on top of the Berlin Wall, wondering whether this was the same thing as the Iron Curtain, and knowing that a display of such joy could only mean that what had stayed hidden behind that wall was merciless.

Curious to see how a society driven by an unrelenting search for the ideal could become so invalid, she had packed her studio and house into a rented storage space. Made an agreement with a gallery for an exhibition on concrete-block housing and Soviet architecture, and signed a contract with a publisher for a coffee-table book on the same. Aware that this was a project tinged with schadenfreude, she was tempted to compare the photographs to the high-rise commission housing that was dotted around Melbourne's inner suburbs. To foster a feeling of us and us, rather than us and them. But would anyone care? Did she? She doubted that the people who lived in the buildings would ever read her book — it was as much an exercise in futility as the buildings she tried to capture. She felt as though everything she attempted had been done before; her efforts to quell the emptiness just made apparent its existence.

Arriving at Potsdamer Platz, she almost laughed aloud.

The entire complex was a hero shot. All soaring ceilings and polished facades, it was a tribute to capitalism and its ability to bring people together through consumption. She was almost twenty years too late and wondered if she was ever going to catch up.

When she thinks about growing old with Andi, she is happily resigned. She looks at his profile as he watches television. The newsreader is speaking too fast for Clare to understand, and she has given up trying to decipher the words. Instead she faces Andi and tries to see him as the stranger he so briefly was. She remembers an elderly couple she once photographed, their unsteady steps held on film forever.

It was the end of winter, and she had been sitting in one of Melbourne's public gardens. The sun possessed the tiniest amount of heat as it fell through bare branches, alighting upon two men who were preparing a flowerbed for planting, arranging potted seedlings so that they fanned out from the central fountain like bicycle spokes. Lighting a cigarette, she had marvelled at the crispness of the unfurling smoke. She had been up all night working and was feeling fuzzy, yet the day placed everything sharply in focus. If ever a day was set for premonitions, this one was it. It was the sort of clear, overwhelming morning where bright-eyed people could see forever, and it was then that she decided she would leave Melbourne and see what life was hiding for her over the horizon.

The city's buildings jostled behind trees, looking as though they had been cut out of cardboard and propped up for her amusement. From a rotunda the sound of two people rehearsing a song could be heard. An accompanying cello pulled their voices into the day, retreating every time they reached the end of the chorus and, with a pause, returned to the beginning.

The elderly couple had walked by, supporting each other, feet shuffling along the sandy path. They looked at the ground and measured each step, taking no notice of the bare flowerbeds, the stunted rose bushes. The man's felt hat sat precariously on his head: 'jaunty,' women would have said fifty years ago. They seemed oblivious to the chill of the day, buttoned up in their long tweed coats.

She had waited for them to pass before standing on the path and photographing them as they shuffled away. It was a lazy shot, but when she developed it later, she could see it was better than anything she had done in a long time.

Looking at the walls of Andi's apartment, she wishes that they were covered with proper family photos, framed and legitimate, a lifetime of memories.

'Do you look like your father?' she asks him. She wonders who Andi might become as he ages.

'I guess so.' He glances up from the television. 'We are both tall.'

'What about your mother? Do you take after her?'

'No.' He switches off the television with the remote. 'Why do you want to know who I look like? I look like me.' He reaches over to her and tugs at her arm. She moves along the couch, rearranges herself to lean against him.

'Do you have any photos of them?' She wants to see his resemblance in somebody else. He doesn't answer her. 'Andi?'

'No, no photos.'

'Are you close to your parents?' She feels his body stiffen.

'Close enough. I see my father sometimes.' He nudges her away, stands up from the couch. 'Are you hungry? I might make something to eat.'

As she listens to him clatter about in the kitchen her appetite deserts her. She has not seen either of her parents in such a long time; the homesickness settles in.

~

The second time Clare left Andi, she hoped that he would follow. She had spent the morning photographing the Palast der Republik, the building dwarfed beneath the cranes being used to dismantle it. While the palace's bronze-tinted glazing remained, there was no sign of the bowling alley, the parliament rooms or the spectacular foyer dripping with one thousand bauble light fittings — nicknamed 'Erich's lamp shop', the guidebook had told her. It was the last building on her Berlin itinerary, but she wasn't quite ready to leave the city. Retracing yesterday's steps, she found herself back in the bookstore, where she squeezed past the Sunday readers perusing cookbooks and headed straight to the art monographs.

And there he was, bent over the very Klimt book she was coming to buy, his lips pursed in concentration and his shirt tag poking out, beckoning to his dishevelled hair.

Put the book down. She willed him to turn around and notice her, but he continued to read. *Put it down.* She loitered by the nearby shelves, noisily picking up and replacing a book. She was not sure what she would say if he glanced her way, but in a city of strangers she was determined to make some kind of connection. Since meeting him yesterday, she had been unable to eject him from her mind; her daydreams knew no bounds. It was just a kiss. She was lonely. But surely loneliness is as good a reason as any to talk to someone? Not quite. In need of pretence, she stepped behind him, reached for his tag and tucked it inside his jumper. Her hand brushed his neck. He turned.

'Your tag,' she said, by way of excuse.

Andi's forehead creased: the international sign for confusion. Or anger. Facial expressions are perplexingly duplicitous. She reached to her own neck, pulled at her own tag by way of demonstration.

'Ah, thank you.'

She thought he would put the book down, but he just turned back to the table. Did he not recognise her? Her face burned: the international sign for embarrassment. She wanted to tear the book from his hands, to keep its pristine pages closed against the light. She wanted to have the composure of Klimt's women and their lack of dimension. She wanted to be painted in gold leaf and empty her eyes until there was nothing left to be read in them.

'That's my favourite,' she said. Adele Bloch-Bauer, her gloves drawn up over crippled hands.

He was silent, flicked the page. A customer squeezed behind Clare, and she found herself pressed up to Andi. Sandwiched, she waited as the customer pulled a book from the shelf then stepped away. Instead of stepping back, Clare remained pressed against him, her hands resting on his shoulders. Could he feel her heart beating?

She stood behind him for almost five minutes. She said

nothing. He said nothing. The moistness of her breath caught in his clothes and clouded back at her. She could feel every part of her body where it touched his. The book and Andi were both things she could obtain, she was certain of this. Yet as the minutes passed and he did nothing to acknowledge her presence, her certainty waned. The heat of him crept through his clothes like an invitation. Her breasts perched neatly beneath his shoulder blades. The left blade poked her left breast each time he reached for a page. Her breast and each page moved in perfect unison. When he reached the end of the book, he went back to the front and began flipping the pages again. She wanted to know whether he was smiling. She stepped back, waited for him to turn to her. When he did not, she walked away.

Engulfed by her palpitating heart and racing mind, she left the bookshop, breaking into a run as she crossed the street. What had she been thinking? Why did she not act like a normal person and just say, *Hello, how are you?* But the world was ambivalent to her private anguish. The sun was setting behind clouds, shop signage asserted itself from the dusk, and the dark lifted up from the asphalt road. Unsure where she was going, she slowed to a walk. The tree-lined street soon passed parkland, and she contemplated waiting out her flush of emotions on a bench. She looked back the way she had come. Did she hope that he would follow? Or did she just want a fast escape? Envious of the cyclists who flew by, their wheels skimming the road, she fantasised about knocking one to the ground, swinging her leg over the saddle and pedalling far away. Why didn't he say anything to her?

The housing blocks gave way to a strip of bars and cafes

where punters crammed in close to one another around tables littered with beer glasses. Recalling the impassable existence of Andi's body squashed against her own in the bookstore, she pulled out a chair at an empty table and waited for something to happen.

One beer, she decided. She would wait for him for the time it took her to drink one beer, and then she would leave. But when her beer came it was slightly flat, immediately destroying any illusion that she was curating a perfect moment. He wasn't going to come walking down that street, and why should he? She thought about things too much. She wished someone would take away her thoughts, wring them out and pass them back, clean, fresh and renewed. Perhaps it was time to go home.

Clare's face broke into a smile as he approached. He hurried the last few paces, flung the book onto the table and dropped himself heavily into the chair opposite.

'I do not like Klimt, you know.' His own words were halting, as though he did not want to give them up. Around them people laughed and waved their hands about, a parody of conversation. 'I think his work is indulgent.'

'Everyone thinks that,' she replied, looking down at the book, rather than at him. 'Because you've seen his work on coffee cups and greeting cards. But when you look at it properly, you see the way his people exist on a different plane. They're real. They're oversaturated with the moment he has put them in.'

She was more than he remembered. He felt tension he had not even recognised leak from his shoes to the pavement, relief rocking in its wake. That morning Clare had appeared in his mind as a series of flashes, a stop-start animation of yesterday's meeting. The mess of her hair that clashed so badly with the pink pipes. The green stitching that skipped around the wrists of her jumper. The way she threw her head back when she laughed. And so he had walked towards the Spree rather than his apartment, crossed the river and headed back to the bookstore.

The book she had been looking at was sitting exactly where she must have discarded it the day before, and he had hesitated to pick it up. When he did, he had turned its pages slowly as though hunting for clues. He had always dismissed Klimt as being excessively decorative and flat, but looking through this book, he realised he had been presumptuous — he had never seen the artist's drawings. Thin lines depicted languorous bodies; sleeping women embraced.

'Your tag.'

And there she was. Tucking his tag into his collar, her hand fluttering over his shoulder and falling to her side.

'Thank you.' He had looked back to the book. Had he conjured her up?

'That's my favourite.'

He stopped flipping pages, and Clare pushed up against him to get out of a customer's way. Trying not to breathe too deeply, Andi had turned another page. *Put your arms around me*. He had stared down at the page, a drawing titled *Two Lovers*. The man's endless shoulders. His back a wavy line, rolling hills. The woman barely seen behind him, her body mimicking the man's. He should have returned the book to the shelf, faced her and taken her in his arms, one fluid movement. But he could not bear to move and create that momentary gap between them.

Wordlessly, she had stepped away and left the store. Why had she not waited for him to say something? Book in hand, he had followed her to the exit. The security system beeped at him, accompanied by the shop assistant's questioning eyes, and he hurriedly paid for the book.

He had walked for ten minutes before he saw her, hurrying up ahead, but he kept his distance, stayed back until she was seated.

'I think, Clare, that I am in need of a beer.' He looked away, searching to catch the eye of a waiter and, even in that moment, feeling that he was taking something from her.

'You will find, Andi, that it is flat,' she said, mimicking his own cadence. 'But I think that it will not matter.'

As the cold of the evening set in, they wielded their conversation like fencing swords. He dodged her attacks, and mounted challenges, each answer part of an adjudicated performance. When the conversation stopped, Clare looked at her watch, and he knew he could not let her away just yet.

'Shall we have something to eat?' When she nodded, he stood and offered his hand. 'How about I make you dinner?'

As she got up, he pulled her in close to him. He wanted to trace his finger along the straggling line where her hair parted. Instead he took her other hand, bringing both together so they were entirely encased between his own. He noticed that her eyes were grey, and nodded because this seemed right.

Clare wanted to postpone the inevitable. Yesterday she had met him on a street corner, today she had shadowed him in a bookstore and tonight she would follow him to bed — but not just yet. As Andi went to the kitchen for another bottle of wine, she rummaged in her bag for a pouch of tobacco. There was not very much furniture in the room. A couch and an armchair sat on a green rug as though lolling about on a grassy island. A television stood in the corner, and a nearby trestle table nursed a stereo and neatly stacked records. The floors were stripped to their boards, the walls bare. Beyond a table stacked with papers, the kitchen opened off at the end of the space, a bench forming a waist-high divide.

She crossed to the window and rolled a cigarette, the smell of unlit tobacco cutting through the room. Afterwards it would linger in the nooks but now, before it began smoking, it smelled like spring. She smoked a smoke; it smoked. What an unusually useful word. You could drink a drink, but it could not drink itself. Lighting the cigarette, she took a deep breath to the back of her throat. It was the slight dizziness of the first drag that she hankered for the most. She would be happy living on first drags for the rest of her life. Most things were like that. The first kiss, the first fuck with someone — so different from all those that came after. And yet how quickly they all became the same. A downhill slide to mediocrity. Though an uphill slide was difficult to imagine. Why did words that usually seemed so normal seem so questionable now? Aware of English being Andi's second language, she found herself scanning all her words to make sure they made sense, editing out all that were colloquial or confusing.

'Do you mind?' she asked, waving her cigarette when he came back into the room.

He shook his head and filled her glass before moving to

the stereo. She pulled the window handle, but it did not move. Locked. The night sky was pallid with the lights of the city; the television tower stood above its stunted neighbours like a candle on a birthday cake. With her head against the glass she tried to see the ground five storeys below, but the light did not quite reach, rendering the courtyard a bottomless sinkhole.

'In a desolate way, it is beautiful. You agree?' he said, coming up behind her, slinging his arms around her waist and resting his chin on her shoulder.

'Yes. Beautiful.' She blew her smoke towards the window, a futile gesture — the smoke rammed against the glass where it seemed to hang, flattened and motionless, like a bedsheet drying on a still day.

'I'm glad you like strawberries.'

Andi whispered it into her ear, his breath tickling at her neck and sending a buzz down her spine. As she turned to face him, he plucked her cigarette from her hand and dropped it into his wineglass on the windowsill. Stripped of its distraction, she felt combative.

'Do you really grow them?' she asked, ducking her head to avoid his kiss. Passing the linden tree in the first courtyard earlier, its last leaves clinging to the branches, had reminded her that it was the tail end of autumn. Could strawberries be coaxed from the ground at such a time of year?

'Does it matter?' He kissed her, his arms creeping beneath her shirt, vanquishing all thoughts of strawberries.

In the bedroom, they fumbled and clawed at each other's clothes, falling to the bed as they tried to undress without letting each other go.

Then, just as suddenly as he had begun, he leaned back, his

hands withdrawn to his hips. 'Wait.'

Her body was singing, crying out to be touched, but he climbed off the bed, leaving her lying there. She shuddered, like machinery too quickly shut down, and in response he lifted a finger to her, requesting pause. Bending to the bed, he unzipped her boots and pulled them from her feet. Trailing his hands up her legs, he slid his fingers beneath the waistband of her undone jeans. She reached for the yoke of his shirt, wanting to lift it over his head, but he shirked away. Nullified, she dropped her hands to her side. She was so entranced by Andi's purpose that it suddenly seemed ridiculous to reach out and grab at his body.

She lifted her hips in compliance, and he guided her jeans to her knees, tugging at one leg at a time until they came free. He kneeled astride her then, pulling her into a sitting position and relieving her of her shirt before letting her fall back to the bed. She reached to touch him, but it was as though her arms were not long enough.

'Be patient.' He smiled at her, bending down to kiss her stomach.

She felt like she was on an operating table, surrendering her body to the responsibility of others. Goosebumps broke out along her side as he ran his hand up her bare leg. From toe to fingertip she could feel her hairs standing alert, and as he got up and finally began to shed his own clothes, longing broke out across Clare's body like spot fires. She wanted him, and his composure only fuelled her impatience. She had been expecting the usual instantaneous give and take of these situations, real-time gratification dissolving the inevitable doubt that accompanied a one-night stand, not this kind of enforced hesitation.

Undressed, he walked across to the doorway and turned off the light.

'No, keep it on.' She did not want to tell him that she had a fear of the dark. That unable to see where she was going, she worried about never being able to go anywhere. She would rather see him, see what they were about to do.

'You know exactly what you want, don't you, Clare?' he said, silhouetted in the doorway.

And because she knew it was expected, and because it was so immediately true, she replied without pause, 'You.'

He flicked the light back on and returned to the bed. They fucked as though it was a test to later be examined on, composure abandoned along with their clothes. She felt deeper in the bed than she possibly could be; that it was Andi who was both holding her down, and setting her free — a bubble rising to the surface. Yet when it was over and they pulled apart, she could not help but feel relieved. The thing they had danced around all afternoon was done; she had nothing owing.

His voice broke the silence. 'It's funny, don't you think, that we come to this?'

She wished she was already asleep and not obliged to take part in this dissection. 'How do you mean?' These conversations that happened afterwards had once intimidated her; she always felt as though her answers were delivered off-key. But now they simply irritated her. She did not want to discuss what they had done; not yet, when they had just finished the doing.

'Well, yesterday, there you were reading in the square, and now we are lying here naked.'

'But we are still strangers,' she said, casting her mind back, then realising. 'You saw me reading? Where? Near the concert hall?' She lifted her head to look at him.

'Of course. That's why I came to talk to you.'

It made sense, but she detected a flutter of apprehension. She had assumed he just happened to be standing beside her at the intersection, strawberries in hand. This revelation meant something, she knew, but sleep beckoned and she hoped he would say no more. Cold, she reached to pull the quilt up.

'No, wait.' Andi grabbed her hand in his own.

'But I'm freezing.' She reached for the sheet again.

He grabbed her wrist, held it beside her body. 'No, really. Wait. When you get very cold and then cover up, it is even better.' He looked at her. 'I promise.'

'Okay.' A shiver crept up her leg, ready to pounce. She tried to imagine that it felt exquisite, but she could sense her body slowly becoming stiff. She tensed her knees, not wanting to move too much and stir the air around her. She released her kneecaps and the left one began to twitch uncontrollably as though it was jogging up and down to keep warm. She clenched her knees again, trying not to think about how cold she was, resulting only in thinking about how cold she was. Finally she gave in, curling her body to huddle against Andi's. But he gave off little warmth, just enough to remind her that the rest of her was cold. She reached for the quilt and pulled it up.

'So, what is next?' His voice was borne through the air to one of her ears, travelled as vibrations through his chest to the other.

'You will turn off the light, and I will fall into a deep sleep?' Please, please let her sleep.

'And after that? What then?' He shifted her off his chest, and slipped out of bed to switch off the light. 'What about love?'

His disembodied voice floated from the end of the bed, trailing behind him as he climbed back in beside her. Did he really say that? He could not be serious.

'Love?'

'Will it come next, do you think? For us?' He slipped his arms about her as he spoke, and despite the warmth, she thought about getting out of bed, dressing and leaving. She closed her eyes and waited for sleep to take her.

One of Clare's breasts is larger than the other. It droops a little more. Her left one. His right. He is watching her move through a series of stretches, and it's making him feel lazy. She raises her arms above her head, grabs the elbow of one and holds the pose. As she does it, her breasts lift and come together, but even so he can tell one is slightly larger. Perhaps it is because she is right-handed. Is she right-handed? He tries to picture her reaching for something, or eating, but he cannot recall her hands. He does not think he has seen her write. Is it that she has nothing to write on or nothing to write about? He feels he knows her body better than he knows his own, yet he does not know whether she is right- or left-handed. If he bought her a notebook, would she make it into a diary? Document each day they spend together, muse about the future? Would she mention him at all?

'You have one breast bigger than the other.'

She looks at him. Says nothing. Drops her arms and then lifts them again, grabbing the other elbow. She is wearing a pair of his boxer shorts, and each time she stretches her arms, he can see how she has rolled them over at the waistband to keep them from falling down.

'The left one.' He wonders whether it has always been that way. He has not noticed it before. It sits lower than the other one. Just a little. Not much. Enough to notice if you're looking closely. He likes to scrutinise her; there is so much to see. She is like a new person every day.

'I know.'

'Oh.' He thought he was telling her something new.

'Most women do, you know.'

'Really?' Now it is she telling him something he did not know. This is why he will never tire of her. She asks him sometimes when he might get sick of her, and no assurance he gives ever seems to convince her that it's just not possible. 'So you are not symmetrical.'

'No. No one is.'

He contemplates this.

'Is that a problem?' She sits herself down on the ground, one leg placed straight out from her body, the other bent, and reaches for her toes. She looks like she is preparing to go for a run. She says it is one of her favourite things to do, and he thinks maybe he should buy her a treadmill — she would like that.

'I'm not sure.' He wonders if the perfect woman would have the same-sized breasts. Clare is strangely removed from her body. Sometimes when he sees her crash her hip into the table or misjudge the distance between herself and the bed, he wonders whether she is aware of her body at all. It is only when she is doing something like this — stretching, or yoga, or handstands — that she seems to pay her body any attention. Even then she treats it as a machine, something to be serviced.

'Would you like me to do something about it?' She stands

in front of him, her left breast cupped in her hand, questioning.

'Perhaps.' He wonders what she could do. 'But it might be what makes you perfect.'

'I could lop it off, like an Amazon warrior. They were rumoured to cut off a breast so they could fire a bow and arrow more accurately.'

'Really?' It makes sense. Breasts would be in the way. But it seems a lot of effort.

'Well, probably not. They probably just bound them.'

'Bound them?'

'Like Chinese women's feet. Broken up and packed away.' She comes over to where he is leaning against the windowsill and mimics his stance. The sill thrusts her hips forward, an invitation. 'So which one?' she asks as he turns to her.

'Huh?'

'Which one would you cut off? The small one or the large one?'

'Neither. I like every bit of you equally.'

When he kisses her, he feels her breasts flatten against his chest.

~

The third time Clare left Andi, the moon was sliding from the sky. As she extracted herself from the bed, Andi breathed on through his dreams. This was what she loved each day, this moment of possibility before the rest of the world caught up. Naked, she could be anyone right now. A businesswoman perhaps, about to slip into pantyhose and a suit that would crackle with static assurance as she trotted confidently down the stairs. An athlete about to attack the day, prove what her body was capable of.

She walked across the dark hall to the kitchen, a room so incidental with nobody in it. She recalled her grandparents' kitchen, dominated by a long table that could seat ten, more if you squashed into the reclaimed church pew that pressed against the wall. When all of her aunts and uncles were home, the kitchen was raucous, a battle zone. Younger cousins would slip beneath the table when they finished their lunch, clamber out from beneath the forest of legs and escape to the openness of the backyard. She would often wish she could do the same, feeling trapped as her family talked on through the afternoon. Instead she found herself sitting still, smile fixed, utterly bereft.

As she stood in this stranger's kitchen, wondering which cupboard held the glasses, that same feeling came crashing down upon her, landing with a thump in her chest, nausea making her reach for the sink. She drank from the tap, letting the water run about her face and neck, the indifferent smell of the metal calming her twitching stomach.

Back in the bedroom she watched Andi, his arm flung above his head, his lashes shivering on his cheeks. He was beautiful. It was pride she felt at having slept with him, a feeling she would never admit to another. She tried to dress quietly though every movement seemed to call out for attention. She never liked waiting for men to wake up. She would rather leave and be a memory that could be returned to. If she stayed, she would become her own bad habits, her stale morning breath, her repeated stories. It was all so very ordinary. She took her boots to the front door, bent to put them on. Would he stir? Call out her name, beg her not to leave? And if he did, would she stay? She liked to think she was strong-willed, but knew that if he woke, she would not walk out that door. Embarrassed by her neediness, she would not let him see it.

Down the stairs, two at a time, and she was swishing through the courtyard leaves that masqueraded as snow in the faint morning light. The air was sharp, winter just around the corner. Once on the street she pushed out her stride and her legs thanked her for it. Perhaps later today she would go for a run, sweat out the excesses of last night.

Connecting the dots on the metro map, she headed back to the hostel and gathered her things. She had been in Berlin almost two weeks and had photographed everything she wanted to. It was time to move on.

Once she had showered and packed, the day had started for everyone else. Trotting down the U-Bahn stairs she tried to keep out of the way of closed-faced people heading to work. The man at the hostel said all trains to Dresden left from the Ostbahnhof, so she found herself repeating the morning's cross-city journey in reverse. She was glad to be on her way.

When Andi woke, she was not there. He threw back the sheets, scissoring his legs, as though he might find her snuggled like a cat in the warmth at the end of the bed. The water pipes were silent; he could hear no footsteps. He held his breath, warding off a false reading. She was gone.

Pulling on yesterday's clothes, he could smell the sex and sweat that clung to him. Still buttoning his shirt, he stood in the doorway of the living room. Was it only last night that he had been right here, wineglasses in hand, watching her roll a cigarette? He had wanted to climb inside her mind, to understand exactly what she was thinking. She had moved so quickly about the apartment; he was certain that if he took his eyes off her she would cease to exist. And so she had. He had found himself following her as she moved from couch to bookshelf to window, a street mime copying her for cheap laughs. She had kept edging ahead of him, throwing her voice over her shoulder like a cape, and he found he could not quite keep up with her, as though the language delay was translating to the physical.

He grabbed his jacket and slammed the door shut behind him, fumbled with the keys in his hurry to lock it. Where would she have gone? Did he have any hope of finding her? The courtyard was too cramped a space to break into a run; he skidded across it and threw himself against the entrance doors. On the street, people marched by on their way to work, and he fell into step with them. His heart was beating so fast it felt as though it was growing inside him: it threatened to break out of his chest and scatter the morning commuters with its bloody shards.

He tried to commandeer his thoughts. Where was Clare planning to go today? She had told him of her travel plans, and he had listened in the way people do when the information does not concern them. Had he not actually thought she would be going anywhere? Or had he not thought he would care? He picked up his pace, headed towards the city. She could not be too far away. What time had she gotten out of bed?

Dresden. He broke into a run. She had said she was going to Dresden, that she wanted to photograph the buildings that had been put back together like a puzzle. Which meant she would be taking a train from the Ostbahnhof. He could catch one, too, he could follow her to Dresden and ... And what? What was he doing? He could not chase her down; he would never find her. But still he ran, his feet slapping against the ground, a stitch stabbing at his side. At the station he barely waited for the doors to slide apart. He burst onto the concourse, conscious of his heaving chest, his expanding heart. He stared blindly at the departures board, the letters swimming about in a code he could not recognise, before running across the hall, dodging the travellers coaxing their wheeled bags. Stopping at the first platform, he looked out across the tracks. And there she was, waiting for him.

'Don't leave.'

The morning after the night before and there he was again. As he came lurching up the ramp to the platform, he looked more bedraggled than she remembered. Her stomach was burning — his presence or sudden hunger? She never could differentiate between her mind's attraction and her body's needs.

'Come back with me.' He delivered his plea with the now familiar jerk of his head, indicating somewhere both nearby and far away. She waited for the question mark, but it did not appear.

'No.'

'Why not?'

'I can't stay, Andi. I've got things to do.'

'Like what?'

'My photographs. The exhibition. The book.' She was touched, and certainly tempted, but she wasn't going to stay — this wasn't part of the plan. She shrugged, apologetic, and tried to change the topic. 'Don't you think train stations just cry out for drama?' Annoyingly, her voice wavered, and she tried to bring the situation back under her control. 'Always scenes of parting. And desperation. Like Anna Karenina wanting to stand back up at the last moment.' The soaring ceilings, the architecture that acknowledged these places as gateways to worlds of more possibility. Flying had appropriated the romance of travel, and budget airlines had killed it.

'Not always,' he replied.

He looked despondent, standing so close yet so separate, and she felt responsible. She knew nothing about this man, she didn't want this connection. And yet she waited for him to reach out and take her hand, to make her stay. But he just pushed his hands deeper into his pockets, and she strengthened her resolve.

'Just stay for a while.' He sounded like a whiny child, and his eyes, which should have been pleading, were accusatory. 'Last night … it was fun.'

With that, her compassion dissolved. It was hardly a declaration. She turned away, wishing that the train would arrive. She wanted to kiss him goodbye and climb aboard. *Clickety clack, don't look back.* It was getting messy, this liaison. It was taking on too many locations.

'So let's leave it like that, Andi.' She refused to look at him, to play his games. Fuck, she was so hung-over. She could feel the station leaning in on her, an overbearing parent waiting for her to confess to some playground crime. Why didn't he touch her? It was disconcerting; it was as though he was not real.

They stood there in silence, each refusing to look, to hold, to walk away. Each wanting the other to force the decision.

'Come back with me, Clare.'

He moved to hug her, and she thrust out her hand, wanting to force him into an awkward goodbye clasp. But he reached higher than she expected, grabbing her upper arm and squeezing. She could feel each individual finger pressing down. Later that night she would look at the bruised imprint of his fingers on her skin and wonder if he needed to be quite so forceful.

'I want you, Clare. Stay.'

'But I want to be away.'

It was the idea she had clung to from the moment she left that crowded kitchen of her childhood. That kitchen drenched with so much sunshine and goodwill that it dripped down the walls and pooled on the floor, causing everyone to slip and slide and crash into each other. She could see them all still there, grabbing at each other for support, laughing as they fell over, helped each other up and fell over again until they were all in a heap. All of them like pick-up sticks not ever wanting the game to be over.

'Everywhere is away from somewhere else.' He squeezed her arm again, the pressure pulling her into the moment.

The sun was cutting through the glass beneath the awning; she felt as though it was chasing them up the platform at speed. Her hangover headache pounded at her skull, teasing her heart to beat faster.

'Please stay, Clare. I really *like* you.' His emphasis on the word made them both blush like teenagers. 'I want you.'

Who could argue with being wanted? In a blaze of clarity,

she saw how simple it was — he would care if she left, and there was no one in Dresden to care if she arrived.

'Okay.'

And in response came that smile running across his face like an incoming tide. When they kissed the taste of him shocked her with its familiarity, so much so that she wondered whether it was, somehow, exactly the same taste as her own.

'Let's go.' He took her hand, pulling her up from beneath all the other pick-up sticks, and not one of them moved.

As the leaves begin to unfurl on the city's trees, Clare keeps her eyes closed and pretends to be asleep. She breathes long, deep and even, listening to Andi go about his morning rituals. The sound of his frothy spit falling into the basin, coffee bubbling on the stovetop. She wonders whether he looks at her as he goes in and out of the room, to the bed, the bathroom, the kitchen. She doesn't dare open her eyes to check. Intent on the order of things, he is conservative in his morning movements, as though he may be taxed on too many trips between sink and breakfast table, fridge and bathroom.

Just before he leaves, he comes to the bed. She hears him pause by her side then feels his grip on the sheets, and they are pulled down to her ankles. The cool air licks across her back but, lying face down, she does not move. With one knee on the bed, he rests his palms on her shoulders before laying himself down upon her, mimicking the length of her body. His knees jut into the backs of hers. His hips are cushioned by her bottom. Despite being much taller than her, he seems, at these moments, exactly the same height.

Flattened beneath him, she feels more present than at any other time during the day. She can feel him along the length of her body, and the weight of him, the stillness of him, calms her. Like this, he cannot hurt her. She can hear his breathing. She wonders whether the earlier smells of coffee and toothpaste were real, or whether they were imagined precursors to this. He bites softly on her earlobe. The goosebumps sing up and down her arms.

'I'll see you tonight,' he whispers, then gets up, takes his bag from the floor and leaves, closing the door behind him.

She lies still on the bed. With his weight removed, she feels light. In this way, every morning she is her very own zeppelin.

When she does get out of bed, she switches on the television. The deep voices of the newsreaders, who never seem to get too excited about anything, encourage her to feel that today is going to be significant. Something is going to happen, they assert with a firm nod. She watches the abbreviated news stories scroll across the bottom of the screen, the English words waving at her like old friends, while the German words slowly become familiar. The multitude of capital letters no longer make her feel as though she is being shouted at. From the newspaper, she cuts out individual letters to make ransom-note poetry. Poetry about the kitchen sink and the grey shrinking view from the apartment window. About the wide land back home, and grass that is never greener on either side. When the ink becomes too smudged to make out the letters, she cuts out more. She can only use the headlines because the other print is too small.

In the long afternoons, she reads the poetry aloud. Demanding the attention of absent crowds, she performs it in bombastic ways that she would not dare to attempt if other people were present. In Budapest she spent a night in a tiny bar listening to poetry. She understood nothing of the language, allowed the unfamiliar sounds to rain down on her until she was slick with the musicality of it. It was not a spoken-word night as she knew it; there was no underlying desperation to remind the audience that poetry as an art form was entertaining, relevant, important. Instead, it was proud literary cabaret: the darkened room, people gathered round the tiny tables, perched on bentwood chairs, smoking, drinking and wallowing in the sea of words. She performs her poetry as though she is back in that room, as though no one can understand a word she is saying, but they do not care, wanting her sounds and listening with rapture.

In the evening, he goes through the sheets of paper, smoothing their curled corners. He reads closely, asks questions. At first, she thought he was making fun; her answers then were curtly monosyllabic. She cringed at the way he enunciated each word, the way he repeated each line with a different emphasis. But she continues to cut out the letters, to shuffle them about into constructions, to glue them in place and dry them by the radiator.

She dreams that there are no more words left in the world. That the authorities have come to her door, knocked, and politely informed her that she cannot use any more letters. Told her that there will be no more newspapers — the population is getting too upset at all the bad news so they will not be printing any more. They tell her that she must recycle her recycled poems, and she does, cutting them up and gluing them down until the letters become ghosts on the page, haunting her with reminders of what has been lost.

~

'Can we walk back along the Wall?' Clare called out to him, pointing at the strip of graffitied Wall that ran beside the river. Andi had paused outside the Ostbahnhof to phone the school and plead that he was too ill to work. He was almost disappointed that the receptionist took his excuse without question. *Actually, I met someone*, he wanted to tell her. *It all started in a bookstore. No, in a park.* But the receptionist just wished him well and hung up.

'It's not really on the way.' He hitched up Clare's bag — the straps were cutting into his shoulders.

'There's no rush is there?'

Of course there was. He wanted to be fucking her. To have her back in his apartment, where they would not have to consider anybody else.

'I just want to get you home. Far away from those mischievous trains that want to whisk you away.'

'I thought you might want to show me your city,' she said, waiting for him to catch up to her and taking his hand. 'I am a tourist after all.'

'There will be plenty of time for that.' He squeezed her hand and could barely believe it when she squeezed his back. He began walking towards his apartment, refusing to let her go. 'Anyway, that bit of the Wall is not real.'

'How do you mean?' She stopped. 'I thought it was the last bit of the Wall still standing.'

'Well, it is. But it's not what it was really like, not how I remember it. There were two walls, with the death strip in between. This bit of wall was on the East side; you could never graffiti it — it was kept completely blank. All those paintings are from after the Wall fell. It's not what it really looked like.' He tugged her arm, made her keep walking.

'How old were you when it came down?' she asked.

'Twelve.'

'What was it like, living like that?'

He shrugged. He never knew how to answer this question. Nothing he could say ever seemed to be the truth. It couldn't encapsulate how normal it was, how definite. How East Germany was a world built on ideas rather than money, that, beneath all of the bad, there was some good. People from outside could never see that.

'It was just how it was. When I was born, the Wall had been up for twenty years. Everyone thought it would be up for a hundred more. It was just the way things were. But it all changed faster than anybody expected.'

'It's odd,' she said. 'Most people feel as though their childhood happened in a world so far away that it doesn't exist anymore. And yours actually did.'

'I guess. In a way, it was like a childhood for everyone — the government was like a parent.' He walked faster, knowing that she was only just keeping up but aware that every minute they were out here, she might change her mind, return to the station. 'Not that parents always know best.'

'But they usually have their children's best interests at heart.'

'True,' he agreed. 'They wanted to produce a society that was as perfect as they knew how. But in the end they screwed it up — just like parents do to their children.'

46

'You can't blame parents for everything. We all have to grow up at some stage, don't we? Childhood will always hold the attraction of innocence, but it's not a way of living. I suppose the Wall coming down was like a massive teenage rebellion.' She pulled her hand from his and stopped walking as she swept her hair up, tied it with a rubber band from her wrist.

His own hands twitched, impatient. He wanted her, wanted to be home.

'Don't you wish you could just go back to being a child though?' he asked. 'Someone else making all the decisions for you?'

'You're like Peter Pan. The boy who never wanted to grow up.' She grabbed his hand; now it was her pulling him forward. 'I can't see you in green tights though.'

Laughing, she lifted his hand to her lips and bestowed a kiss, which he returned. He remembered the story well enough; it was one of his father's favourites.

Finally, they reached his building, and he led Clare once more through the courtyard and up the stairs. As he unlocked the door, she pushed him aside. 'Race you to the bed!'

Hours later, standing naked in the lounge room, Clare pointed at the television tower. 'It's kind of weird, isn't it, to know just about everyone in the city has the tower in view.'

'It's not what I'm looking at.' He came up behind her, ran his finger down her back.

'It's kind of like a lonely pervert. Looking into everyone's living rooms.' She stepped away from him, leaned a hip against the window frame and began rolling a cigarette. It was as if she didn't even notice she was naked, yet that was all he could see.

'Have you been up there?' she asked.

'Not since I was little.' He remembered waiting in the queue, and then the elevator operator standing between him and his father, the material of her dress tickling his face. He had squatted to the floor as the elevator climbed, and his ears felt like they were going to burst.

'Let's go now,' she said.

He didn't want to leave the apartment. That he had to work tomorrow burrowed at his consciousness. If they went out there, it would take time. Time to go up the tower, to come down again, and to come home. And then once the time was all used up it would be tomorrow, and he would have to leave Clare and go to work. But her enthusiasm was infectious, and soon he found himself at Alexanderplatz, queuing for the lift, tickets in hand.

'It is only going to disappoint you, Clare.' Standing beside her, he twisted a lock of her hair around his finger, marvelling at how each strand was a different shade of red or brown. 'It will be full of tourists and screaming children.'

He was wrong. When they arrived at the top, it was busy but hardly overwhelming. They circled the deck slowly, and he pointed out landmarks. From here, it looked like any city. When he had last visited, the Wall dominated the view, a gash across the city stitched together with guard towers and raked sand. At some places, the gap between the Wall was over a hundred metres wide; at others, it looked as though you could leap across.

'It could be the end of the world, couldn't it?' she said.

The setting sun cast elongated shadows across the city, the twilight emphasised by the observation deck's tinted glass. At the bar he ordered drinks. A portable radio crackled through top-forty tunes, and he was bewildered that, despite being inside Germany's biggest aerial, the reception was so bad. Clare must have felt sorry for the barman, who kept trying to tune the radio, and she distracted him by ordering elaborate cocktails in her tourist German.

By midnight he was drunk on Japanese Slippers, and even he could tell his conversation was nearing incoherence. They fell into the lift, and as they plummeted to the ground, he wished there was a gentler way. The train home rattled his insides, and he was relieved to be back on solid ground as they walked the few blocks to the apartment.

Up five flights of stairs, Clare behind him, out of breath as he searched for his keys. Pocket after pocket. They kept eluding him, and he couldn't remember which pockets he had checked and then he had to start his search again. Clare leaned against the wall, raised her eyebrows, and once more he felt the panic that if he didn't find them soon she would be down the stairs and on a train. There. He pulled his keys out at last and let them inside.

In the kitchen he filled two glasses of water and swallowed them both down before refilling them and taking them to the bedroom. He could hear the shower running. Kicking off his shoes, he lifted his shirt over his head, tossing it on the floor on the way to the bathroom. He drew back the shower curtain. She was so blank. Immediately, he went hard. Colour flushed her body where the hot water struck.

He had never fucked in the shower before. Pulling her to him, he did not know if he would be able to hold her up. She wrapped her legs around him, he pressed her against the wall. Her skin was hot beneath his hands, against his chest. He pushed. She pushed. He pushed harder. Every move of hers was a challenge to him.

He could feel her resistance and he wanted to reach her there, where she stopped being soft. He grunted and pushed. The water was deceiving; it slid between them, taunting. Just as he felt like he was getting closer to her, he would find himself further away. And then it was over. Clare, her back against the tiles, slid down until her feet hit the ground. He let go of her, his knees shaky. He could not feel the water on his face, only the sweat forming beneath it. He turned the taps off, leaned back on the wall beside her, and they stood there, dripping, not touching.

Catching his breath, he reached for her hand and pulled her to him. 'I wish this moment never stopped,' he said. She was warm on his front, the tiles were cool on his back. 'If I could have one wish, that is what it would be.'

She kissed his neck, and he felt her hot breath creep over his shoulder. 'I would wish to never want to be anywhere else.'

The words muffled in his ear, confused, and he tightened his grip as though to squeeze their meaning out of her. *'To never want to be anywhere else*,' he said. 'So you want to always be here?'

'No.' She pulled away from him, kissed him and stepped out of the shower. She seemed so composed, yet he could only just keep standing. Surely she was as drunk as him? 'Well, in a way. But what I want is to live in the moment. Don't you think that would be amazing? To never be wondering what will happen next and whether it will be better than this?' She passed a towel to him, took one for herself. 'I wish I always wanted to be wherever I am.' She started vigorously drying her legs, her arms.

He watched, transfixed, her words piled in his mind. He wanted to fuck her again, to have her never stop talking, to keep on drying herself as long as he stood there. The room shook in time with the movement of her towel.

'But maybe we are always looking forward to something else,' he said. He followed her out of the shower, concentrated on keeping his balance. 'I don't think there is anything wrong with that. Not if there are things to look forward to.'

'It is impossible to be present in the present.' Her words floated out from beneath the towel and eventually her face followed. She threw the towel at him, and he caught it.

'I suppose,' he replied, shaking his feathery head.

'Which is exactly why it is the one thing that I always want.' She grabbed his hand, pulled him into the bedroom. 'Apart from sleep.'

When she woke she lay still, hoping the throbbing in her head would be alleviated by her inaction. It was. She opened her mouth, stirred her bloated tongue. Reluctantly, she opened her eyes. The bedroom window was translucent: it presented a muted swatch of sky, giving only a hint of the weather and the time. She became aware of the weight of the blankets, the sheet twisted around her shoulders, and she pulled back the covers, inviting the cold air of the apartment to clutch at her bare skin. Relief. She did not remember going to bed last night. Sitting up, she swung her feet to the floor. Her hair was matted — she must have slept with it wet. Remembered the shake of the shoulder, the kiss on the cheek, and a promise to be home no later than four.

God, they must have drunk a lot. She recalled scenes like a game of memory, tried to match them with sense. The views from the television tower observation deck, Berlin laid out like a distant galaxy. That barman who kept trying to woo her with lines from songs, his voice sailing above the static of the radio. Andi surveying the barman's attempts, smiling beatifically. *Ugh*. No wonder she felt rotten: cocktails.

Head pounding, she walked to the bathroom. The apartment had retired beneath a grey shroud. In the shower, more vague memories of last night returned. She soaped her body all over. She felt tender — they must have been so drunk, gone at it hard. Was the steam from the shower beneficial? Or was it making her feel dizzy? She turned off the water and, as she stepped onto the bathmat, she remembered: they had sex in the shower last night. She grinned. No wonder she was sore.

Feet wet, towel tight around her, she walked back to the bedroom. Aware of every movement of her body, she tried to dodge its demands. She wanted orange juice. An apple. She needed to feel cleansed on the inside. She would go for a walk, get some air. Maybe buy something for dinner. The regular little housewife.

She dressed and liberated her jacket from last night's clothes. Without Andi's presence, the apartment was numbingly impersonal and, considering her current state, she was glad. Being unable to tell what kind of person lived there meant she did not have to make judgements on her own presence. The books and records gave a clue, but most of the surfaces were bare, the recipients here and there of everyday possessions. Used wineglasses. A cigarette lighter. A newspaper. There were no photos, not even free cafe postcards stuck to the fridge. In the bedroom, her own belongings crept out across the floor, attempted to colonise the space.

She swung her camera bag to her shoulder, checked that her wallet was inside. Her phone battery was flat, and she debated whether to leave it charging, but the only people who had her number were on the other side of the world, sleeping. She imagined all the people she knew sharing one enormous bed. Sighing, shifting their weight, searching for the cool creases of untouched sheets, surrounded by the rustling of polite dreams. It was a relief to toss her phone back on the bed. Friends texted occasionally to ask her where she had been, where she was going, but somehow her answers never seemed to match the colour-saturated anecdotes they wanted to hear, and the messages dried up.

In the kitchen, she checked the fridge and hunted out a string bag from the drawer. Cutlery always in the top drawer, kitchen utensils in the next. Tea towels in the third and bags and cling wrap in the fourth. An organisational system as universal as the Dewey decimal.

She was at the front door and reaching for the handle when she realised she did not have a key. Damn. She couldn't go out; she couldn't get back in. A rushing in her ears. The silence was — what was it? Not quite encompassing. It was absent. It was almost suffocating, as though the noise had left, taking the air with it. She wondered why she had not noticed before. There — the hum of the fridge. Her heart slowed, she was holding her breath. The creak of the building shifting. Her own shifting weight. Her head hurt. Perhaps she should go back to bed. It was the sort of day when, if she wasn't forcing herself into the studio, she would usually call a friend, drink a pot of tea and while away the afternoon until the ache subsided.

Fuck, this was really annoying. She took off her jacket: she was sweating. She tried to open a window but could not. In the bedroom she kicked off her shoes and flopped onto the bed. The sheets had already taken on the familiar, sour smell of intimacy. She wanted to be angry with Andi for not thinking of her need for a key. But she expected he felt as hung-over as she did, and he'd had to go to work. Poor thing.

She lay on the bed for a while then moved to the couch. The apartment did not seem so very spacious and light anymore. The ceiling dropped, the walls shuffled in. She closed her eyes and imagined she was far away.

She remembered being in the car when she was young. Waiting with her sister for their mother to come out of the supermarket. Clare's sister had unbuckled her seatbelt, climbed into the front passenger seat and shut the vents. They weren't supposed to touch them. Everything on the dashboard was off limits. In fact, being in either of the front seats was off limits without Mum or Dad about. Her sister locked the passenger door then reached across the driver's seat and did the same on that side. With two hands she pulled on the window handle, winding it up.

'If we make it airtight, it will be like space,' she had said. Clare had pictured the dark night sky, constellations she could never identify. 'Zero gravity. If we have no gaps we will be able to float, like in space.' Her sister nodded her head gravely.

'Pass me the tissues.' Her sister pointed at the tissue box on the parcel rack. Clare did not move. She recalled so desperately not wanting to be involved. Her sister rolled her eyes and climbed over into the back seat where she grabbed the box of tissues. Back in the front seat, she began stuffing the tissues into the air vents.

'You'll break them,' Clare had said, concerned. She hated it when things broke. It was not the being in trouble that she minded. It was seeing the broken thing in front of her, useless.

Her sister ignored her and, taking a gulp of air, lifted her arms from either side of her body. Clare almost expected to see her float up to the roof, to bounce lightly off the windows. She didn't.

'It doesn't work.' Clare felt it was her duty to pronounce this, to allow the experiment to be over before their mother came back.

But her sister just looked at her with annoyance. 'It will.' She began stuffing the tissues around the windows.

'Don't waste them,' said Clare. That was what Mum always said when they used too many tissues. Her sister continued to ignore her, determinedly stopping the gaps.

She could not remember how it actually ended. They didn't float, she reasoned. Mum probably came back and bawled them out for using all the tissues, laid down new rules for being left alone in the car. Always the reassessing of rules.

She wished there were more rules now. A rule that Andi had to be back at a definite time. A rule that if he went out he had to leave a key. Relationships established their rules quickly: the permissible and the unthinkable were soon separated, the latter quarantined until further notice. And when the rules were broken, the relationship was weakened. Snap, snap, snap, until it fell over. So maybe a relationship without rules was not so bad. No rules to break, no way to end. The logic was astounding. She opened her eyes, tried to shake the overly earnest thoughts from her head. She found that her mind always raced when she was hung-over, while her limbs trailed behind. It was no use: she needed to get outside.

Maybe there was a spare key somewhere. She stood up from the couch and began hunting. There weren't many places to look. She rummaged in the bowl by the bedside lamp. Nothing in the drawer of the bedside table — some papers, two buttons, three condoms, a paperclip, some tweezers. The bathroom held only bathroom things. The kitchen, too, lived up to its name. She walked along one of the floorboards in the hall as if it was a balance beam in gymnastics class. In the bedroom she took four small steps from the door to the end of the bed, where she flopped down again, defeated. The foot of the bed. Why was it hands but not foots? Feet but not hend? What the fuck was she going to do all day?

'Don't just lie there.' As she said it, she could almost hear her mother's voice. She got off the bed, put her shoes back on, and picked up her jacket and bag. She had not really thought about her mother in years. Not in this way, the memories colliding into one another like dodgem cars. And she didn't want to think about her mother now; she just wanted to be here, no future, no past. Fuck it, she would just go out. If she stayed out long enough, Andi would be home from work when she got back.

The front door was locked. She twisted the latch and pulled, but the door did not open. Perhaps there was a trick to it. She pulled again, but the door did not open. She was confused: she had no trouble leaving yesterday morning. And then she saw, lower down on the door, the second lock. A deadbolt. Had he locked her in?

She felt slighted, wanted to kick something. She gave the door a half-hearted nudge with the toe of her shoe. It was one thing not to be able to get in. But not get out? How could he have forgotten she was here? How could he have locked her in? She kicked the door again, harder, and a scuff mark appeared like a rebuke.

It was not even one o'clock. At least three hours until Andi came home. She let out a groan of irritation and resigned herself to waiting. He was going to be so embarrassed when he got home. In the kitchen she mixed up a bowl of muesli, made a coffee in the stovetop percolator, oily and dark with use. If it did this to stainless steel, what did it do to her insides? She took her coffee to the living room and tried to concentrate on choosing a record, but all she could think about was Andi. His smile, the way he mooched rather than walked. He haunted her like a pop song: she couldn't get him out of her mind. How did he forget her long enough to lock the door? It was almost insulting. Annoyed at his oversight, she still smiled when she thought about how mortified he would be when he returned. Sipping her coffee, she turned the pages of the Klimt book. It was just a door, she reminded herself. A simple door, in a regular apartment. It was not Fort Knox. Where was Fort Knox? If Andi had a computer, she would Google it. It sounded American. It must be something to do with the Civil War. A short, strong American name. Square. Democratic. It was a quarter past one. Hours of confinement to go.

Andi watches ribbons of rain flap against the window frame. The bulb of the television tower is lost in fog; the lights announcing its tall presence flash faintly, like hovering UFOs.

'I'm bored, Clare.' He looks over to her. She is lying on her back, reading a book he gave her, her feet pressed up against the radiator.

'Clare?' He can hear the whine in his voice. He is jealous of her ability to get lost in a book. Whenever he buys her one, he feels like he is giving her permission to ignore him. 'Clare, what can we do?'

She doesn't answer him, so he walks over to the stereo, flips idly through the records. The tips of his fingers seem extra sensitive, the record sleeves tickle. He bounces on the balls of his feet. It's the being cooped up, the closed walls. His father is the same, cannot abide small spaces. They used to head to the country on weekends. Go hiking through woods, across fields. It should have been idyllic, a father-and-son outing in bucolic isolation. But Andi remembers it being so suffocatingly purposeful. They would get off the train at whatever station his father had chosen and begin walking. When they ran out of roads, they would tramp through fields, animals shuffling away from the path. Andi would try to keep up with his father's long strides by settling into a quick trot. But as the day wore on, he would drop further and further behind as his father disappeared into the distance.

When eventually he caught up, his father would be laying out their packed lunch beneath some shade.

'You made it!' he would say, ruffling Andi's hair. He always seemed so pleased to see him, making Andi wonder why his father had worked so hard to leave him behind. After lunch they would walk back to the train station together, at an easier pace. His father would point things out. The names of trees, the different types of clouds. He would ask about school, his favourite subjects. He would tease Andi about when he was going to find himself a girlfriend. On the train home Andi would sleep uneasily, and when the rolling carriage jerked him awake he would see his father staring out the window. As dusk crept by and turned everything navy, it seemed his father was shrinking. He would slump lower and lower in his seat, his bony knees jutting further into the aisle, his eyes never closing.

'Here we are then,' his father would say, as the train pulled into their station.

They would walk back to the apartment in silence: Andi, his father and the week ahead.

'Let's make something.' Clare has tossed her book aside, rolled onto her stomach. Her feet dangle in the air, misshapen in a pair of his socks.

'Like a cake?'

'No. You bake a cake. I mean … I don't know. Like a house or a model. A structure!'

'But what with?'

'Well,' she says, standing up, ready to take charge. 'What about newspaper?'

Following her instruction, he begins rolling the weekend newspapers into thin tubes.

'I used to do this as a child.' She tells him about the house she grew up in. The fruit trees in the backyard, the swings hanging between tall gum trees. The track she and her sister wore into the ground from riding their bicycles around the yard in circles. How they would build jumps for their bikes and rollerskates from brick and scraps of plywood. Build them higher and steeper until one of them eventually hurt herself enough for their mother to come outside and tell them to stop.

He tells her about how he once wished for siblings. His memories are all of school and the Young Pioneers. Of organised sports and camping. He spent so much time with his friends and classmates he was never lonely, but he mainly remembers activities that were supervised and always for the good of something other than himself.

'Even then it never felt real,' he says. 'It was always mediated, as though even childhood had to be commandeered to the socialist cause.'

The afternoon trundles on. They compare more childhood memories, sing jingles from advertisements and ABBA songs. The rain falls, and their newspaper tower rises. He doesn't recognise his fingers, busy and smudged with newsprint. He cannot remember the last time he spent an afternoon making something.

'It's more Pisa than Eiffel, isn't it?' he observes, as they flop onto the couch later to admire their handiwork. The tower is made of tightly rolled tubes, taped together to make a pyramid base. As it got taller and thinner, it had started to bend; despite the reinforcements, it seems to be performing a curtsey to them. The peak is decorated with a splay of newspaper, its fronds falling open like fireworks. Impressive for an afternoon's work.

He runs his hand up and down her thigh — it gives beneath his touch. Forgiving. He feels like he could endlessly knead it and it would keep bouncing back like yeasty dough. He wishes she was not wearing jeans; he wants to feel her skin. The metal button at her waistband carries the heat of her body, and he slips it from its buttonhole. She lifts her hips, tugs her jeans to her feet, and his hand is on her skin. She lifts one socked foot and then the next from her discarded jeans while he continues stroking. Inky fingerprints mushroom across her thigh. She keeps her legs pressed together, a neat valley forming in her lap; the reddened lines that cross her legs like highways on a road map are hidden from view. They do not need to be mentioned. She lays her head on Andi's shoulder; he knows she has closed her eyes, is leaving him for somewhere else. He picks up one of her hands and places it on his own leg. Directs it up and down. When he stops, so does she.

'Don't you like touching my leg, baby?'

He feels her tense beside him. She does not like being told what to do. But he wants to feel her hands on him, he wants to be covered with her newsprint fingerprints.

'Of course I do,' she replies. Her hand recommences its brushing back and forth.

~

As he taught his way through the day, Andi resorted to a mantra: *she is home, she is waiting for me*. He repeated the phrase to himself under his breath, over and over, breaking only to give instruction to his classes. He wished he did not know his students' names, that they would appear only as an indistinct sea of pimples and petulance. He felt exposed, all of his inadequacies on display. She did not need him. She would not be there when he returned home. When he left the apartment that morning, he had wanted to run back up the stairs, make her promise not to go anywhere, to be there when he returned from work. But she would have thought him desperate. Was he? He herded students through grammar exercises, corrected pronunciation. His answers were concise. *She is home, she is waiting for me.* The students nodded in agreement: his explanations of the nominative case made sense to them. They laughed at his jokes and didn't groan at the amount of homework he gave. When the final bell rang, he bolted. *She is home, she is waiting for me.*

Peter called out to him as he collected his things from his locker in the staffroom.

'Are you coming for a drink, Andi?'

He tried to avoid Peter's expectant gaze, did not want to explain about Clare, not yet. 'I've got to get home.'

'Come for a drink with us. We have something to celebrate.'

Jana appeared by his side, nodding encouragement.

To celebrate? He did not want to know, did not want to share in anyone else's joy.

'Sorry, I really have to go. We will celebrate soon, okay?' He clapped Peter on the shoulder and hustled his excuses ahead of him out the door.

When he realised he had forgotten his scarf, he did not go back. What if she wasn't there when he got home? He stopped walking and leaned over the gutter: he felt ill, his body punishing him for last night's cocktails. What if she had already left again for the station and he had not been there to bring her back? A woman passed by, her dog sniffing around his ankles. A cyclist threw him a dirty look, not sure if he was about to step out into the street.

He started walking again, hurried down the steps to the station platform. The air was dry and heavy. People shuffled about like pigeons, heads down, retreating from the day, a sea of brown and black and denim. Would she at least have left a note, her email address? He willed the train to go faster, cursed the slow opening and closing of the doors at each stop. A man sat down beside him and bit into a kebab. It squelched like a kitchen sponge, the smell of garlic sauce filling the carriage.

It was a relief to finally head out into the open, to cross the road to his street. There was no way she would still be there; she could not possibly feel this way about him. She did not seem to need him in the way he needed her, in a raw, irrational way. She liked him. She wanted to fuck him, of that he had no doubt; her body met his with possessive audacity. But was that enough?

He opened the door. She was still there. The relief bucketed down on him like a practical joke. He had been running this scene through his head all day, readying himself for the disappointment of her absence, and yet here she was, she was waiting for him.

'You locked the door, Andi! I've been stuck in here all day.' Hands on hips, she stood her ground like a child.

He had locked her in? He looked from her to the door to the keys in his hand. Ran through his morning routine — and realised.

'Oh, Clare! I'm so sorry! I did not think. Why did you not call me?' He rushed towards her, grabbed her hands, a literal begging for forgiveness. He had locked the second lock as he did every morning when he left. What was he thinking?

'But I don't have your number. I was stuck here. It was like being a prisoner.'

'I am so sorry, Clare, I really am. I did not even think about it. It was routine.' He was horrified. He could not believe he had been so careless.

'At first I thought I wouldn't be able to get back in. Then I realised that I couldn't even leave.' She shook off his grasp, attempted to assert her annoyance.

'And I spent all day just trying to convince myself that you were real and would still exist when I got home.' He reached for her again, squeezed her arms as if they were a pair of soft toys, almost expected a responsive squeak. 'I *am* sorry, Clare. I really am.'

He wrapped her in his arms, rocked her from side to side. He wanted to have her right now, to feel her bare skin against his, but when he moved to kiss her she pushed him away.

'Stop!' She was laughing as she batted away his needy hands. 'Let's go out — I need to get out of here.'

'Of course you do.' He wished she did not. 'Shall we go and get something to eat?'

Her assent was a lingering kiss, which he savoured while she went to gather her things together. He ducked into the bathroom, his heart bopping in his chest. *She is here, she is here, she is here.* He splashed his face with water, sluicing away his too obvious relief and trying to dampen his desire.

'Ready?' She appeared in the doorway as he dried his face on a towel.

He rubbed doggedly, taming the corners of his smile, which wanted to jerk up in triumph at every opportunity. *She is home, she is waiting for me.*

Andi suggested a Turkish restaurant around the corner, but she did not want to sit down just yet; she needed to walk off the day's confinement. As they crossed the railway lines she packed away her bad humour and tried to concentrate on what he was saying. She was surprised when the River Spree came into view, and they walked its banks towards a mammoth sculpture of three men who looked like they were about to embrace. As with Melbourne, where the Yarra runs like a mud-brown afterthought, she never thought of Berlin as a river city.

With relief, she felt time begin to slip. They crossed a turreted bridge that an artist had engaged in an endless neon game of rock, paper, scissors, and left the main road to head into parkland. She always found herself so very aware of time — of its passing, of its residue, of its promise. It was one of the things that initially attracted her to photography, the way it managed to hold time still. There was a peacefulness about the final image that belied any urgency to capture the moment. When pressing the shutter button, she felt as though she was protecting her subjects from their future, allowing them to stay at their best. Trying to explain this to Andi, she was aware of how unintentionally worthy it sounded and she let her voice trail off.

'But what is wrong with the future, Clare?' He did not look at her as he asked, gave her the space to answer. 'Are you afraid of what might happen?'

'Not afraid,' she replied too quickly. He would think she was lying. She had never needed to be afraid, never been in any kind of danger. 'But just so very aware of it.'

She tried to speak as Andi did, selecting each word carefully to isolate its meaning. 'The future crowds out the present. If I knew the future would be no different from now, I would just enjoy it. But I never know, so I can't ever stop wondering.'

'It's enjoyable enough if you ask me.' He pulled her into a kiss then stopped. 'Why do you close your eyes?'

She opened her eyes to find him scrutinising her face. 'I don't know.' She had never thought about it before. If she had, she would have assumed that the person kissing her was closing their eyes also. 'Because your face is too close to focus on?'

'But don't you want to see?'

'I already know what you look like.' She kissed him again, her eyes closed. She opened them. He was staring at her, and she broke away from him, laughing. 'It's distracting! I need to close them so I can concentrate.'

Abruptly, he let go of her hand and began walking up the path. Was he angry? She was not going to run after him. She stood still, unsure of whether she had just made a decision or whether he had.

'Come on. I want to show you something.'

Walking backwards, he beckoned to her. She hesitated, then hurried to catch up. They walked past the memorial, caught only glimpses of the heroics of the Soviet soldier, saved child in arm, swastika crushed beneath boot.

'Look,' he said. A Ferris wheel peeked from behind the bare trees, autumn's fall bringing it into view. 'There's a whole theme park here. It's been closed for years.'

They came to a tall picket fence, and he gave her a leg up. She scrambled over the top and let herself down the other side, her feet sliding without purchase on the slippery wood.

'Are you sure this is a good idea?' she said, as he landed heavily beside her.

'Shhh.' He put his finger to her lips. 'It's patrolled by security guards.'

The forest was completely overgrown. The last of the daylight struggled to drip through the canopy; bracken snapped beneath their feet. But even in the murky light of dusk, she found the park's incongruity becoming. A Viking ship tipped in a deep curtsey at the foot of the Ferris wheel; a herd of swan-shaped pleasure boats crowded the chestnut trees like the gathering of a lonely hearts' club. Further on she stifled laughter at the sight of toppled dinosaurs and little cars that must have once travelled on tracks, their passage now halted by the impenetrable undergrowth. The cars were shaped like moustached men, their windscreens decorated with painted spectacles and their roofs sporting brightly coloured hats. Above, purple egg-shaped capsules hung from a track that wound through the trees, ivy anchoring each one to the ground and, just beyond an enormous big top, a rainbow cat's gaping mouth welcomed the tail-end of a rollercoaster. He led her into the big top where the red and yellow canvas reined in the last rays of sun, bathing the circus ring in an apocalyptic orange dusk.

When it was so dark she could hardly see Andi's silhouette, let alone his expression as she mimed amazement at each neglected ride, she let him lead the way through the jungle-like scrub back to the fence. It was only when they were safely on the other side that she looked at him and burst into laughter.

'It's amazing, Andi! I can't believe all of that is right here. I have to come back in the daytime with my camera.' Her words ran on, tumbling out of her mouth in her excitement. 'It's like a dedication to all the fun that people are not having. Those little cars were so adorable! And the swans, they're so forlorn.' She paused, waited for him to tie his shoelace. 'But there's something kind of hopeful about it all, don't you think?'

'Perhaps.' He took her hand, and they began to make their way towards the city. 'But not for the owner. I think he was done for drug-running in Peru.'

And for some reason neither of them could stop laughing at the misfortune of the funfair owner, even when it started to rain and they had to sprint through the park and across the bridge. Splashing through the streets, Andi pointed out favourite places and endeavoured to make his neighbourhood her own, and briefly she dared to think that perhaps this was what life had in store for her. Under the influence of such unfettered happiness, she wondered why she had not believed in fate all along. Was it too sentimental to start now? As the rain pattered in fat drops, they slunk into a bar and, legs pressed up against each other's, fingers entwined, they participated in their own private call and response deep into the night.

She wishes she had fresh flowers, but the ones Andi bought last week had browned and drooped within days and were consigned to the bin shortly after. It is winter in Berlin: no flowers are growing anywhere nearby. She guesses the ones he bought were imported from Africa, cut, refrigerated and flown to Germany. They were probably in shock, the blooms no longer sure what season it was, whether they were supposed to be open or closed. It was little wonder they only lasted a couple of days. She strips the bed and makes it with clean sheets, tossing the dirty ones into the laundry hamper in the corner. In the living room she clears mugs and glasses from the coffee table, slips records back into their covers. She takes the broom from beside the fridge and sweeps the floors. They need to be mopped, but she does not have time today.

In the kitchen she takes milk, eggs and butter from the fridge; flour and sugar from the canisters on the shelf. She wants to make a cake for Andi's birthday but must do it by guesswork and memory — she didn't want to ask him to translate a recipe and ruin the surprise. As she measures and stirs, she is assaulted by memories of her mother doing the same. Each birthday, Clare was allowed to choose a cake from the *Women's Weekly* children's cake book. She and her sister would crowd over the book, turning each page slowly and considering the merits of each cake. There were trains and aeroplanes, dolls in full skirts, pirate ships. The swimming-pool cake, with its chocolate log walls and blue jelly surface was a favourite, as was the racetrack in the shape of a number eight, decorated with Matchbox cars. One year, Clare helped her mother make a cake for her father. It was shaped like a guitar: the strings were made of strips of liquorice, and the tuning pegs were chocolate bullets. He was so impressed, he had not wanted to eat it; he even got her mother to cut it up. 'Would you look at that?' he kept saying, shaking his head. It was his last birthday. He died three months later, a car accident on the way to work, and when his next birthday came around, none of them knew what to do, or whether to do anything at all.

For Andi, she will keep it simple. His kitchen doesn't have an electric beater, and by the time she has creamed the eggs, butter and sugar her hand is aching. She sifts in the cocoa and flour, adds the milk and keeps stirring, tasting as she goes. She lines a pan with baking paper and pours the mixture into two shallow trays, which she places in the oven. Once it has baked and cooled she will slice the cakes and shape them into a letter 'A'. She knows that he will be pleased.

When the timer goes off, she takes the cakes from the oven and leaves them to cool. She was surprised to find icing sugar when she hunted through the kitchen cupboards last week, and she mixes it with water, crushing the lumps against the side of the bowl. She slices the cake and arranges it on a chopping board. The two cakes did not rise the same amount, so she has to cut one down. It's fiddly work, and she is running out of time — it all took a lot longer than she expected. When she starts applying the icing, she finds the cake crumbs get caught up in it. The cake looks nothing like the professional surfaces of her mother's. She scoops on more icing, and it drips down the side of the cake, pooling on the board, but finally it is finished. Exultant, she places the cake on the dining table. She has achieved something at last; her day has been worthwhile.

~

Andi's weight lifted from the bed, dropping her deeper into the mattress. Shivering, she tried to move her body beneath the covers, but her arms were too heavy, they could not grasp the blankets, and she gave up, curling her body to warm herself. Her limbs were aching. She was so incredibly tired; she felt as though she had danced all night. Her head was soft, and still she could not open her eyes. She slept. When she woke she could hear Andi's footsteps about the apartment, and she pictured him following close behind. Step, step, step. He opened the bedroom door.

'Andi?' Her voice did not sound like her own. 'Did you leave the key?' She felt his lips on her forehead; she supposed it must be a kiss and she forced her eyes apart, tried to find his face in the dull light.

'Here it is.' His face was closer than expected, and she pulled away as he flashed a silver key at her, putting it on the bedside table. 'I will see you tonight.'

Her mousetrap eyes snapped shut, and she tumbled back into sleep.

When she woke again, her mouth felt chocked full of cotton-wool clouds. She must be coming down with something; she probably caught it in the rain last night. Coughing a papery cough she retrieved her knickers from the floor and pulled on one of Andi's t-shirts. If she were a Hollywood star she would look fresh-faced and fabulous. The t-shirt would hang from her shoulders like haute couture. Instead, it looked large and misshapen. Her breasts lounged ungracefully without a bra.

It was cold in the apartment, and she hunted out a pair of Andi's socks, not wanting the uniform of her own clothes. The floorboards became a skating rink under her feet, and she glided easily across the hallway to the kitchen. As children, she and her sister had wanted to ice-skate, yet Australia was not a land for ice and snow. A rink was set up in a marquee by her town's lake one winter, but it proved a grey, crowded disappointment. The ice was lost beneath a watery sheen, making the whole thing appear an oversized puzzle, and skaters moved about the rink stiff with awkwardness, trying not to see themselves in their neighbours' discomfort. She and her sister had more fun at home slipping about on the polished wooden floor of their playroom in socks, yelling out 'red' or 'green' and trying to catch each other out as they stopped and started.

Now the heft of her body tried to pull her to the floor, but she resisted. At the living-room window, she pressed her face against the cool glass. Below, the courtyard was unkempt, the concrete cracked and uneven. The veneer of the building opposite was crumbling. Andi had told her that the whole building was deserted — a property developer owned it and was planning on renovating it. The practical side of the apartments faced her, pipes like varicose veins and mean, frosted bathroom windows.

The television tower rose above the city in a timeless parody of itself, unconcerned by gravity. It was one of those literal, concrete reminders of the past that she had been photographing, trying to capture within her lens the proud socialist hope for a future already lost. It reminded her of last night's fun park — she would try to get some decent photographs there this afternoon. Reluctantly, she peeled her face from the windowpane. She felt rotten; she should shower. In the bathroom she was careful, as was appropriate in a stranger's abode. She was learning the rules. She didn't want to upend a bottle or let a jar go clattering loudly into the sink. She didn't want to leave pubic hairs on the soap or a wet puddle by the shower. The water plunged from the shower rose, fat and dull, and the steam seemed to fill her as it expanded, pushing her unwilling mind against its peripheries.

Her head spun when she got out, and she let herself sink to the floor. Her eyes drooped of their own accord, and she sat on the bathmat in a cocoon of darkness, waiting. After a few minutes she pulled herself upright and, towel wrapped around, stumbled back to the bedroom. The sheets were cool as she fell into them, and for a moment she thought that might be enough to keep her awake, but then she pulled the blankets over her, drew her knees to her chest and let go.

'Clare?'

She rolled over to see Andi in the bedroom doorway.

'Why are you still in bed?'

Irritation dragged her away from sleep. His question made her feel like a posing teenager. 'I was tired.' She pushed the sheets away, the towel still clung damply to her. 'What time is it? Did you come home early?'

'No, it's almost six. Are you okay?' He sat on the edge of the bed. She watched him reach out to her and saw him hesitate. When he did touch her his hand was cool, like a doctor's.

'I've just been so tired. I think I might be getting sick. I haven't slept that long in ages.'

He tossed the towel to the floor and lay down. She experienced a disorientating moment of déjà vu. Had he lain down clothed beside her before? From here she could see only one of his eyes; it blinked rapidly as though wondering where its partner was.

'It's nice to come home and find you in my bed, Clare. It's like a gift.'

Watching his watching eye, she moved her face closer to his, kissed him on the lips. Lifting the blankets up, she let him into the bed and shifted her body around his. The cool of the outdoors drifted from the creases of his clothes, and she felt him shudder as she slipped her hand beneath his shirt.

He appraised Clare's body with his hands: they swept up and down her length. Like a store mannequin, her body dipped and curved into stillness. Her hot hands crept beneath his shirt, and it was the confirmation that he needed. She wanted him just as much as he wanted her. They tumbled about the bed, and her body seemed to slip through his fingers while her hands grasped at his clothes, simultaneously pulling them off and holding them tight as though she might drift away.

Later they sat at the dining table, and he watched her eat, his own food lying untouched on the plate. He was holding her camera, and as he scrolled through her photos the buildings formed a flip book of Soviet history.

'So did you go out at all today?' He held his breath, waited for her answer, knew what she would say.

She wrinkled her forehead at him, turned her attention back to her food. 'No, I told you. I was exhausted. I slept all day.'

She had decided not to leave. He continued scrolling through her photos. He was right.

'Why buildings?' he asked. He wanted to hear her voice, the unfamiliar accent rippling out across the table, filling the space of his apartment and reminding him that he was not alone.

'Because buildings can lie. People think that they don't — and that photography doesn't lie. But they both do. They manipulate perspective, influence memory. They hide things in shadows, draw your eye away from detail.' Her fork swivelled in her hand like a conductor's baton, pausing to wait for the next beat to continue on.

'You can only be in one bit of a building at a time and a person's eye can only focus on one thing at a time. I like playing on these presumptions. There's so much going on out of the shot, but people refuse to think about that. They think photography is the whole, captured truth.'

Looking through the photographs of the buildings that skirted the cities of Riga and Vilnius, he was surprised by how similar the setting of his own childhood seemed to these places. It was the level of decay more than anything, the crumbling frontages between the uniformly sized windows. These same buildings had already been renovated in East Berlin or were waiting to be revealed, hidden behind builders' scaffolding, their facades being plastered over like the faces of ageing matinee idols.

And then he saw it, why the images seemed like postcards from an indiscriminate time: there was evidence of human habitation but not a single person in any of the shots.

'There are no people.'

'Exactly!' She put her fork down, pushed the bowl away. 'Do you know how long I had to wait to photograph some of those places?'

He scrolled back through the photos; his revelation had made them seem unsavoury, as though they were documenting something that was over, not a place where life was still happening.

'But why? People live here. They use these buildings every day. That is what makes them important. Otherwise they are just shells.'

'But they're not. Buildings make us do certain things. I wanted to cut out all the people so the viewer can't humanise the buildings.'

'What is this one?' He passed the camera to her. It looked

like a manipulated photograph, a stately nineteenth-century building framed by a black border with letters cut out of it.

'It's the Terror Háza in Budapest. A museum for victims of fascism and communism. It's not for the exhibition, but it's kind of interesting, don't you think?'

She described how the black blades cantilevered out from the building's roof to form a verandah, and how the sunlight fell through the letters, casting the word 'terror' across the museum.

'The Nazis and the Soviets used the same building to torture and imprison their enemies. Don't you think that's strange? Buildings matter more than we know.'

'They have them here, too,' he said. 'The former Stasi offices, the prison in Hohenschönhausen, they are all memorials now.'

'What I love about buildings is that they signal civilisation. When they're standing, all is well, and when they're destroyed, it's the end. Knocking them down is a way of deleting history, so those very buildings that people were terrified of at one stage become the ones people visit to face their fears. Have you been to the prison?'

He shook his head. He had never contemplated going to Hohenschönhausen. It was another world, another time. It did not belong to him. Clare frowned at him. He had disappointed her.

'You know what's fascinating? Every city throughout the former Eastern Bloc seems to have them. Museums of terror, of occupation, of genocide, of deportation. And they are often in the very building where the KGB had their offices. Even when the people are gone, the buildings remain. It's sad that

these places exist, but necessary, don't you think? So that people know?'

He could hear the urgency in her voice, the ownership, and something about it put him on edge. 'But don't you worry that it's not your story to tell?' It was not her history. 'You can exhibit your photos, put together your book, but it's not your story, you were not there.' He watched the hurt spread across her face. This is what he wanted. Because he felt like she was lecturing him — she did not know what it was like. She knew nothing about him.

'I'm not trying to make it mine, Andi. I'm just taking the photos and putting them out there. I don't want to speak for anyone — I don't think I am.'

'The buildings will not tell you anything, Clare. It was the people inside who were responsible. People did things then that they would not usually do. You'll never know what it was like.'

She shrugged. 'People can do terrible things to each other. We'll do it again and we'll use the same buildings to do it in. I guess I just want the buildings to tell their story, that's all.'

He focused his attention on the screen, scrolled on through the images. 'There are no photos of you.'

He lifted the camera and pointed it at her, pressed the button. Captured her in that moment just before she smiled, as though her expression was waiting to be issued the command to show him happiness.

'Why don't you have any tattoos?' he asks her.

He runs his fingers across her back as they lie in bed, marvelling at the foreverness of her skin, so white and pink.

Not pink — beige. No, it is something else, a white over red, her greedy skin hoarding the red pumping moistness of what lies beneath. White with a blush, like that of a pig's carcass hanging from a butcher's hook. He pictures a fluorescent pink stamp marking her, stating what she weighs, how much she is worth.

'Because everyone has tattoos.'

'And if everyone says the sky is blue, do you say it is red?'

She furrows her brow at him, purses her lips. 'And tattoos always fade and bleed into blurriness,' she says, refusing to bite. 'Why don't you have any?'

He watches his own hand stroking her back. When he spreads out his fingers, he can cover quite a bit of her. He could draw a line around his fingers, tattoo his handprint onto her skin, where it would wave at her in the mirror every time she undressed for a shower.

'I don't know.' He pictures the tattooist, a stranger, holding his skin taut. 'I have always been too worried that I wouldn't love the design forever. Imagine waking one morning and realising you hate it but you are stuck with it for the rest of your life.'

'It's like cattle branding, isn't it?' she says. 'A way of identifying who owns what.'

'I suppose it is nice to belong to something.' He lies down beside her, pulls her body to his as he nuzzles into her neck. She does not resist — she is a rag doll. 'Isn't it?' he says.

He had wanted a tattoo for a long time. The same permanency that attracted him made him afraid to commit. He recalls sitting in a park, eating an egg sandwich, mesmerised by an elderly man's tattooed feet. At the time, he was studying

in London, always amazed as the office workers stripped their clothes off in the public gardens, worshipping the weak sun in their lunch hour. The man's suit jacket was discarded beside him on the grass; his shoes were unlaced and placed neatly together, the socks laid on top. His feet were almost luminescent in the sun; the blue ink of the tattoos seemed to have melted into all of his crevices. It had taken Andi some time to figure out what the two figures — one on each of the man's feet — were. A rooster and a pig. He had been fascinated: the age of the man, the unexpected discovery of his decorated feet. Later he found out that they were sailors' tattoos, mired in superstition. A pig on one foot and a rooster on the other was a guarantee of a sailor's life: both animals feared drowning so much that they would ferry the sailor to shore as quickly as possible, if only to save themselves.

The more he discovered about sailors' tattoos, the more he wanted one. The anchor that marked a voyage across the Atlantic, the shellback turtle that indicated a crossing of the equator. Twin swallows on the shoulders that told of the crossings of the tropics of Cancer and Capricorn. He did go to a tattoo parlour once, determined to get a swallow tattoo of his own. Desperate with homesickness in the droning buzz of London, he had thought it particularly pertinent. Swallows always come home. But sometimes people do not. In the end, he learned so much about the tattoos that he respected their meaning too much to get one. He was not afraid of drowning, but it seemed like tempting fate.

'Maybe we should get tattoos,' he whispers into her ear. There's no longer any fate to tempt. For a long moment she does not answer.

'There was a couple I knew,' she says, finally. 'They each had a star tattooed onto their wrists, with a tail trailing behind. When they held hands, it looked like the stars were jumping from one arm to the other, round and round in circles like they were being juggled.'

He skims his hand up her arm, sees a jet stream in its wake. 'I have a better idea.' He goes into the hallway and comes back with the satchel he takes to work and searches around in it until he finds a pen. 'Now, don't move.' She is lying on her stomach, and he sits astride her, smooths his hand over her lower back.

'Oh god, not there!' She tries to roll over, laughing, but his weight is too much. He feels her squirm but sits firm, pinning her to the bed. 'I could never get one there! It would be like getting two dolphins swirling around my belly button.'

'Ah, the ironic tattoo position? Hmmm ...' He reaches behind, grabs her calf. 'What about here?'

She kicks her foot. 'No!'

'I know.' He grabs her hand and holds it above her head. Straightaway she seems taller. The hair beneath her arms is strawberry blonde, a washed-out version of the hair on her head. Still straddling her and holding her hand aloft, he begins to write, just below her arm, towards her back.

Her skin gives beneath the pen; he has to press down to get the ink to catch. She doesn't move — is she holding her breath? *Meine*, he writes. It looks like a tattoo immediately, apart from the inky blob on the tail of the final 'e'. The ink takes and holds: it looks like it is embedded within, rather than written on, the skin. He should have done it in red pen, like a meat stamp. *Meine liebe.*

'What is it?' She squirms about, impatient.